Disney's
My Very First Winnie the Pooh ™

Pooh's Scrapbook

Kathleen W. Zoehfeld   Illustrated by Robbin Cuddy

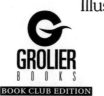

GROLIER
B O O K S
BOOK CLUB EDITION

Based on the Pooh stories by A. A. Milne
(copyright The Pooh Properties Trust).

Printed in the United States of America.

First published by Disney Press, New York, NY
This edition published by Grolier Books, ISBN: 0-7172-8926-5
Grolier Books is a division of Grolier Enterprises, Inc.

"Blah," said Tigger, "I hate rainy days. There's never anything to do."

"Blah," agreed Piglet.

"Well," said Pooh, "we could try remembering sunny days. That ought to cheer us up."

"I remember . . . making castles in the sandy pit," tried Tigger.

". . . gathering haycorns in a basket," said Piglet.

". . . climbing the bee tree for honey," said Pooh.

"Haaaaaaa," they all sighed. Now they were feeling worse!

"Oh, bother," said Pooh. "There must be something we can DO. Think-think-think."

"What if we made a Sunny Day Scrapbook?" said Piglet.

"A book of scraps?" asked Pooh, who was thinking it sounded a little silly, though he didn't want to say so.

"No," said Piglet, "a colorful book, filled with special pictures and words—you know, scraps of memories."

"A memory book! What a clever idea," said Pooh.

They opened Pooh's cupboard and took out a stack of paper—all different colors.

They brought out paints and crayons for making pictures, and pencils for writing.

They brought out scissors and glue and ribbon for putting it all together.

"How do we start?" asked Tigger.

"I think we should tie the pages together first," said Piglet.

"Yes," agreed Pooh. "Then we can draw our memories and cut them out and glue them down on the pages."

Tigger counted out sheets of construction paper. He stacked them together neatly.

Pooh found his hole puncher and made three holes in the side of each sheet.

Piglet threaded the ribbon through the holes and tied it in a bow.

Then they all sat down around Pooh's table and started making pictures of their favorite sunny-day things.

Piglet drew a picture of the time he and Pooh went to Owl's house for tea. Pooh added a paper teacup to the page.

Tigger drew Roo's jumping contest.
Then he cut out a "Best Bouncing" prize.

Pooh drew Rabbit's garden.
He found some old seed packets to add to the page.

"Let's do more!" cried Piglet.

He drew a picture of everyone building Eeyore's new house.

Tigger added some cutout tools and a helpful drawing about how to build a house.

Tigger had fun painting.

Piglet drew a picture of his favorite game, Pooh Sticks. He added some leaves he'd saved from the day he won.

And Pooh drew a yummy picnic with friends!
He added lots of cutout honeypots.

Soon their scrapbook was ready.

"This is so-o nice, we should make a pretty cover for it," said Piglet. "Then it will be like a real book."

"Will these do?" asked Pooh, holding up two sheets of heavy paper.

"Yes," said Piglet. "But they're too big. I'll trim them so they're just a little bigger than our scrapbook paper."

When they were just right, Pooh punched three holes in each heavy sheet to line up with the holes in the paper.

Tigger rethreaded the ribbon through all the holes and tied the bow again.

"Our Sunny Day Scrapbook!" said Piglet proudly, "What a nice thing for remembering fun!"

"Tiggers love rainy days," sighed Tigger, admiring their work.

"They're the best," agreed Piglet.

"Next time it's sunny," said Pooh, "let's make a Rainy Day Scrapbook."

"Yay!" cried Tigger and Piglet. "What a clever idea!"

You Can Make a Scrapbook, Too!

Your scrapbook can be about anything you like: a birthday party, a trip, a holiday, special friends, days at school, your family, your pets, or something you wish and dream for! Ask a grown-up to help you.

You might fill your scrapbook with notes and cards from friends,

photographs, postcards, stamps,

old tickets to movies or shows,

or pictures from magazines.

To decorate your cover, you can paint pictures, glue fabric down, or create a collage with cutout pictures and colored paper.

But remember . . . you can put anything you want in your scrapbook, and you can decorate it exactly as you like it. Because this is your special book!